PEDRO
~ PEDRO IS ~
~ RICH ~

by Fran Manushkin

illustrated by
Tammie Lyon

PICTURE WINDOW BOOKS
a capstone imprint

Published by Picture Window Books, an imprint of Capstone.
1710 Roe Crest Drive, North Mankato, Minnesota 56003
www.capstonepub.com

Text copyright © 2022 by Fran Manushkin
Illustrations copyright © 2022 by Capstone

Library of Congress Cataloging-in-Publication Data
Names: Manushkin, Fran, author. | Lyon, Tammie, illustrator.
Title: Pedro is rich / by Fran Manushkin ; illustrated by Tammie Lyon.
Description: North Mankato, Minnesota : Picture Window Books, an imprint of Capstone 2021. | Audience: Ages 5–7. | Audience: Grades K–1. | Summary: When Pedro receives some money from his grandmother for his birthday, his father suggests that he put some of it in the bank, but then Pedro has to decide what to do with the remainder.
Identifiers: LCCN 2021004208 (print) | LCCN 2021004209 (ebook) | ISBN 9781663909787 (hardcover) | ISBN 9781663921857 (paperback) | ISBN 9781663909756 (pdf) | ISBN 9781663909770 (kindle edition)
Subjects: LCSH: Hispanic Americans—Juvenile fiction. | Money—Juvenile fiction. | Birthdays—Juvenile fiction. | CYAC: Money—Fiction. | Hispanic Americans—Fiction.
Classification: LCC PZ7.M3195 Pcdm 2021 (print) | LCC PZ7.M3195 (ebook) | DDC 813.54 [E]—dc23
LC record available at https://lccn.loc.gov/2021004208
LC ebook record available at https://lccn.loc.gov/202100420

Designer: Tracy Davies
Design Elements: Shutterstock/Freud

Table of Contents

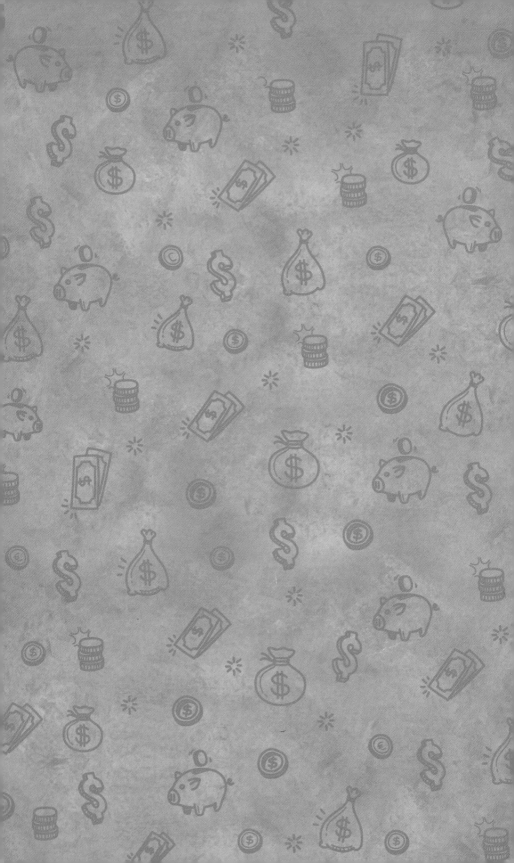

Chapter 1

Pedro's Birthday

It was Pedro's birthday.

His grandma gave him a funny

card. It had lots of money in it!

"Wow!" yelled Pedro. "Thank

you, Grandma. I am rich!"

"I have lots of money too,"
said Katie. "I keep it in a
piggy bank. I love shaking my
money and making it jingle."

"I keep my money in a glass jar," said JoJo. "I can see it when I shake it!"

JoJo asked Pedro, "Where

do you keep your money?"

"I keep mine in a box,"

said Pedro. "I love to count it."

"You can put some money
in the bank," said Pedro's dad.
"It will be safe, and your money
will grow."

"Wow!" said Pedro. "I hope
my money grows as tall as you!"

Chapter 2
Future Plans

Pedro and his dad went to

the bank. Pedro gave them a

lot of his money, but he kept

a little.

Later, Pedro told Katie and
JoJo, "My money is growing in
the bank. Maybe it will grow
as high as a mountain!"

"My money is growing too," said Katie. "I will buy my dad a gold watch. He will never be late again."

"I'm getting my mom a
new car," said JoJo. "The car
will be shiny red, like her
lipstick."

"Cool!" said Pedro. "We
can all take a ride."

Pedro told Katie and JoJo,
"I have a little money to
spend today. What should
I do with it?"

"You should get ice cream,"
said Katie. "Ice cream is a
good way to spend money."

"For sure!" said Pedro.
"I will do that."

Chapter 3
Time for a Treat

On the way to the store,

the three friends saw Roddy.

"Let's play soccer," said Roddy.

"That's a good idea!" said

Pedro. "I can get ice cream

later."

Pedro kicked the ball hard.

He kicked and ran.

Whoops!

His money went flying out of his pocket. The wind blew it away!

"I'll help you find it," said Katie.

"Us too," said JoJo and Roddy.

They looked in the tall grass and the trees. They found all the money!

"Thank you," said Pedro.
"This is a lot of money. I can
buy myself ice cream cones
all week!"

"That's right," said Katie.

"You can have a new kind every day," said JoJo.

"Lucky you," said Roddy.

They began walking away.

"Wait!" yelled Pedro.

"I know the best way to eat ice cream."

"How?" asked his friends.

"With you," said Pedro.

"The ice cream is my treat!"

"Yay!" yelled everyone.

They each had a different flavor. All of the cones tasted cool and sweet.

"Feeling happy is as much fun as feeling rich," said Pedro.

And it was!

About the Author

Fran Manushkin is the author of Katie Woo, the highly acclaimed fan-favorite early-reader series, as well as the popular Pedro series. Her other books include *Happy in Our Skin*, *Baby, Come Out!* and the best-selling board books *Big Girl Panties* and *Big Boy Underpants*. There is a real Katie Woo: Fran's great-niece, but she doesn't get into as much trouble as the Katie in the books. Fran lives in New York City, three blocks from Central Park, where she can often be found bird-watching and daydreaming. She writes at her dining room table, without the help of her naughty cats, Goldy and Chaim.

About the Illustrator

Tammie Lyon began her love for drawing at a young age while sitting at the kitchen table with her dad. She continued her love of art and eventually attended the Columbus College of Art and Design, where she earned a bachelor's degree in fine art. After a brief career as a professional ballet dancer, she decided to devote herself full time to illustration. Today she lives with her husband, Lee, in Cincinnati, Ohio. Her dogs, Gus and Dudley, keep her company as she works in her studio.

Glossary

bank (BANGK)—a business that stores and lends money

flavor (FLAY-ver)—the kind of taste in a food

jingle (JING-guhl)—to make a light clinking sound

money (MUHN-ee)—the coins and bills people use to buy things

shiny (SHY-nee)—very polished and bright

Let's Talk

1. What sort of container do each of the main characters keep their money in? Which one would you choose for your money?

2. How do you think Pedro felt when he lost his money? Have you ever lost something? How did you feel?

3. At the end of the story, Pedro says, "Feeling happy is as much fun as feeling rich." Do you agree with him?

Let's Write

1. Pedro and his friends talk about what they want to buy others. If you could buy something big for someone special in your life, what would you buy? Who would you give it to?

2. Design your own piggy bank by drawing a picture. Write a sentence to describe it.

3. Pretend you are Pedro and write your grandma a thank you note for your birthday money. Be sure to say what you did with it.

Where does a penguin
keep its money?
in a snow bank

What did the football coach say to the
broken vending machine?
"Give me my quarterback."

What is brown and has a head and a
tail but no legs?
a penny

Knock, knock.
Who's there?
Iowa.
Iowa who?
Iowa you a dollar!

When does it rain money?
when there's a change in
the weather

How much money
does a skunk have?
one scent

What kind of money do
Santa's elves use?
jingle bills

Why did Pedro put his
money in the freezer?
He wanted cold, hard cash.

HAVE MORE FUN WITH PEDRO!

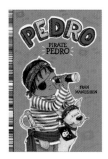